American Horse Tales

North Wind Acres

by Shaquilla Blake

Penguin Workshop

To the horse-crazy phase that I never grew out of, to my family and friends for hounding me to stay on schedule, to my husband for making my love of horses a reality (at the expense of his own sanity), and to every horse-loving kid whose dreams feel too big—never give up.

—SB

W

PENGUIN WORKSHOP
An imprint of Penguin Random House LLC, New York

First published in the United States of America by Penguin Workshop,
an imprint of Penguin Random House LLC, New York, 2022

Visit us online at penguinrandomhouse.com.

Library of Congress Cataloging-in-Publication Data is available.

Printed in the United States of America

ISBN 9780593519356   10 9 8 7 6 5 4 3 2 1 COMR

Chapter 1
A Fantastic Opportunity

"All right, Daija, bring him down to a walk and cool him out," called Ms. Julie.

I patted my lesson pony, Argus, on his neck and whispered a soft "Good boy" before letting him stretch.

I couldn't stop beaming from ear to ear. During today's lesson, Argus and I floated around the arena perfectly in sync with each other. Even now, my body swayed in motion with Argus's walk, and with every inhale that he took, I could feel my calves rise and fall at his sides. As we walked, our breath visible in the unusually crisp September air, I could see that my parents and Ms. Julie were deep in conversation, but I couldn't make out much of what they were saying. It was rare to have both of my parents here to watch a lesson, so I was especially proud of how well Argus and I had ridden.

After a few minutes of walking, Ms. Julie called to me from the opposite end of the arena. As she talked, her bright white teeth were blinding and her russet-brown, poufy afro, which matched her skin tone, glistened in the sun with every move of her head. Ms. Julie, who was dressed in a navy North Wind Acres sweatshirt, tan breeches, and tall riding boots, stood a few inches shorter than my mom and looked much younger than my parents. It would be easy to mistake her for one of the older kids.

"Daija! You can hop down and head out to the barn to untack and groom. Be sure to give him a good currying—you two worked hard today."

I pulled Argus to a halt in front of the arena mirror and dismounted. Swinging the reins over Argus's head, I unbuckled my helmet and shook my black box braids from their loose ponytail. Looking at Argus and myself in the mirror, I admired this beautiful horse, with his copper coat and long, wavy mane. His rich color made my own medium-brown skin seem to glow, and even my gold necklace with the cowboy hat pendant that my mom's dad, Grandpa Joe, had given me for my ninth birthday shined bright. I pulled a peppermint from my pocket and fed it to Argus before leading him toward the arena door and the barn.

"You can put a cooler on him, take him in his stall after you groom, and then meet me in my office,"

Ms. Julie instructed as she held the arena gate open for Argus and me to exit.

"Yes, ma'am," I said, nodding my head. My mind raced as I wondered why Ms. Julie wanted to see me. Had I done something wrong in my lesson? Was I in trouble? I was pulled from my thoughts with a yank on my arm as Argus spooked at the barn cat, Lady, who scuttled between his legs.

"*Easy*," I whispered to Argus as I made quick work of slipping his halter over his head before clipping him to the crossties. I carefully but swiftly removed his tack, gave him a good grooming, and put a fleece cooler on him to keep him warm as his coat dried. Before I turned off the lights and headed to the main barn where Ms. Julie's office was located, I locked Argus in his stall and left him happily munching on hay.

My palms felt clammy, and my heart pounded

in my chest as I knocked lightly on Ms. Julie's door. I closed the door quietly after she granted me permission to enter, and I took a seat in the empty chair next to my mother.

"I was just telling your parents how much progress you've made, Daija," Ms. Julie, with a bright smile on her face, said to me before turning back toward my parents. "I believe that Daija would be an asset to the show team."

The North Wind Acres show team was well-known on the show circuit. Ms. Julie's students always brought home blue ribbons and were some of the best in the state. She was very respected for training with a focus on horse welfare. Of course, I had dreamed of being on the team, but I hadn't thought that I would have a shot for a few more years. I had been around horses since before I could walk, thanks to my grandpa Joe, but I had only started formal riding lessons a few months ago after my best friend, Kayla, had pony rides at North Wind Acres for her birthday. Kayla had been taking lessons with Ms. Julie for almost three years and was already on the show team. My heart raced even faster, and I began to pick anxiously at my nails as Ms. Julie continued.

"What does being part of the show team entail?" asked my mom.

"In addition to Daija's current program of one private lesson a week, she would take two additional group lessons per week with other show-team members, and she would have one more day ride on her own," Ms. Julie said as she pulled a printed calendar page that read SEPTEMBER at the top of it. "We would just need to find which days would work best for your family."

"Four days a week is quite the commitment—

both physically and financially," responded my mom.

"What would we be looking at cost wise?" chimed in my dad. "We have no plans to buy a horse anytime soon."

"You wouldn't have to think about buying a horse now," assured Ms. Julie. "Kids will outgrow their ponies as they advance, and that tends to happen pretty quickly. It is perfectly normal to lease a large pony or small horse for Daija to show. There are plenty of North Wind Acres horses available."

I racked my brain, wondering which of the amazing horses I would get to lease. At only twenty-seven years old, Ms. Julie was considered young to be a trainer with such a big program and reputation, but it spoke to how skilled she was at her job. My mother reached over and swatted my hands apart to stop me from picking at my nail beds. This nervous habit left me with messy-looking fingers and always left my mother with a frown on her face. I sat on my hands to fight the urge to continue picking while I listened intently.

"What are the monthly costs for the show team?" asked my mom.

"A monthly cost of one thousand three hundred and fifty dollars will cover Daija's three lessons and the lease fee for one of the lesson horses. Depending on which shows Daija competes in, the show fees will vary."

I sneaked a glance at my parents' faces. Dad's brow was furrowed as if he were confused, and Mom looked worried. Riding was expensive, and showing was even more expensive, but I wanted nothing more than to be on the team.

"Now I understand that this is a significant increase to Daija's current program in both time and price. However, Daija is one of the most mature and dedicated students in my program. Her willingness to learn and her natural talent are profound and incredibly rare at her age, and I want to nurture those qualities in her. To offset the costs, I would be willing to offer Daija a working-student position."

I couldn't believe what I was hearing—not only had Ms. Julie complimented me, she was willing to let me be a working student! So many top riders had started out as working students or grooms; I sat a little straighter in my chair.

"What is a working student?" asked my dad, leaning in and looking very curious.

"Daija would perform barn chores—help with feeding, mucking out stalls, tacking up the lesson horses, etcetera, in exchange for her weekly lessons and lease of a horse. You would only be responsible for paying show fees and maintenance for her lease horse."

"How often would Daija need to work?" asked my mom.

"We could work out a schedule to accommodate everyone involved. Of course, school is the first priority, so leaving plenty of time for studying and homework is imperative. I require that all of my show-team students maintain at least a B average."

The room became quiet for a minute. My parents appeared deep in thought, and Ms. Julie and I anticipated their responses. As my mom leaned forward to speak, Ms. Julie beat her to the punch.

"I know this is a lot to commit to and not a decision to make lightly. Why don't you folks talk it over first?"

"Sure, that would be great," replied my mom.

"Of course, here's my card," said Ms. Julie, holding a card in each hand for Mom and Dad. "Please feel free to reach out with any questions or concerns." Ms. Julie, standing from behind her desk, turned to me and said, "Excellent riding tonight, Daija. You are making fantastic progress with every lesson. Keep up the great work."

"Thank you, ma'am," I answered shyly. Ms. Julie was a tough instructor. Though she was always happy to repeat things as many times and in as many ways as you needed to understand something, she didn't tolerate excuses or lack of trying.

Ms. Julie and my parents shook hands again before my family exited the office and headed toward our parked car.

"I can't wait to tell Kayla that I'm joining the show team!" I said excitedly as I walked alongside my parents.

"Hang on there, kiddo. Your mother and I have a lot to discuss."

I could feel my excitement start to fade, and it was replaced by worry. Being invited to join the show team was such an honor; what could my parents have to discuss other than when I could start?

As my dad pulled down the long driveway toward home, I pulled my phone from my backpack and texted Kayla with the exciting news. While my parents chatted with each other about dinner and weekend plans, I sat in the back seat and replayed Ms. Julie's words over and over in my mind.

Once I got back in my bedroom, I pulled my cell phone from my jacket pocket and sent Grandpa Joe a text message.

Hi, Grandpa Joe!

7:16 p.m.

My little cowgirl! How are you, Daija?

7:19 p.m.

I'm good—I just got home from the barn. Guess what!

7:20 p.m.

Fantastic—that's good to hear.

7:20 p.m.

It was AWESOME! I rode Argus again, and we just clicked! BUT GUESS WHAT!

7:22 p.m.

Okay, okay, I'll bite. What?!

7:22 p.m.

My instructor, Ms. Julie, offered me a spot on the North Wind Acres show team and a working-student job!

7:23 p.m.

That is EXCELLENT! Well done, Daija. When do you start?

7:23 p.m.

Well, Mom and Dad said that they need to think about it. They are worried that being a working student and on show team will be too much for me to handle.

But I KNOW that I can do it. I wish that I could convince them somehow.

7:24 p.m.

Why don't you show them that you have a plan to handle so much responsibility? You could make a very detailed list for your mother— you know how she loves her lists and plans.

7:26 p.m.

That's a great idea! Thank you, Grandpa!

7:27 p.m.

> Next time we talk, I want to hear that you are officially on the show team!
>
> 7:28 p.m.

> I will! Good night!
>
> 7:29 p.m.

If my parents were worried that I couldn't handle school, being a working student, and riding, I would show them that I could. I began drafting a schedule to show when I would ride, complete my barn duties, do chores, and study. About an hour later, I heard a knock at my bedroom door.

"Come in," I said, still focused on filling out my calendar and schedule.

"Hi, Daija, your father and I want to have a quick chat with you before dinner," said my mom as she took a seat on my bed. My dad followed and sat next to her. I swung around in my desk chair, my heart racing.

"First off, we want you to know how proud of you we are. You looked phenomenal in your lesson tonight, and clearly Ms. Julie sees your progress."

"Thanks, Mom, I felt really great today."

"We understand what a big honor it is to be invited to be a part of the show team. Your dad and I love that you love riding as much as you do, but we're worried that being a working student, maintaining your grades, and riding multiple times a week will be too much pressure on you at such a young age. You are very mature for an eleven-year-old, but we do not want to burden you with having to work to maintain your spot on the show team."

I could feel my heart start to sink as my mom continued.

"Affording a lease, lessons, show fees,

transportation—it is a big commitment, and it just isn't something that we can afford right now."

"You wouldn't need to waste money on transportation!" I chimed in. "I could take the bus!"

"Daija, taking the bus at your age in Detroit is very dangerous," responded my dad. "North Wind Acres is a few miles outside of the city. Perhaps in a few years, but I'm not sure we would be comfortable with you traveling by yourself."

Desperately trying to plead my case, I grabbed my calendar and showed them what I had already jotted down on my carefully drafted schedule.

"I know that accepting Ms. Julie's offer is a lot of responsibility, but I promise that I can handle it. Look at the schedule I've made—it maps out the bus route, days that I would ride, times at the barn that I could work on my homework—"

I paused as my parents' eyes scanned my work.

"This is quite impressive, Daija," mumbled my dad as he continued to read.

My parents were silent for what seemed like forever. They exchanged a glance, and my mom gave a slight nod before they both turned to me.

"If you are going to accept this opportunity and the responsibility that comes with it, there will be some ground rules," began my dad.

"THANK YOU, THANK YOU, THANK YOU!" I shouted as I leaped forward to hug both of my parents, burying my face between their shoulders.

They were chuckling as they recited the rules. I listened as best as I could, but I was mostly imagining myself in the show ring.

"Text us when you leave school and when you arrive at the barn. Homework and grades are nonnegotiable; if your grades slip, riding is suspended. Understand?"

I focused back on my dad's words and nodded a firm yes. I wasn't worried about following the rules and handling the responsibility; I wanted to ride, and I was willing to do whatever I had to do to make that happen.

Chapter 2
Welcome to the Team

It was the start of a new school year, and I couldn't stop checking the clock during the last class period. I had told Kayla the good news about show team as soon as my parents left my room, and we couldn't wait for my first group lesson. We had been talking about it all day at school. But we wouldn't be able to go to the barn together because Kayla was in the extracurricular program, which meant that her last period was an enrichment activity outside of school.

Kayla's mom had scheduled a car service to pick up Kayla and drop her off at the barn on her lesson days, so she would already be there. The clock ticked painfully slowly, and 2:20 p.m. seemed much further away than fifteen minutes. I wondered what the other show-team members were like and what horse I would be riding during the lesson and during the show season. As the bell rang, I closed my binder and quickly exited the classroom toward the study-hall session held in the cafeteria. Show-team practice began at 4:30 p.m., so I had a half hour to get some of my homework done before I had to prove to my parents (and myself) that I could safely get to the stables.

~

As I climbed aboard the number forty-four bus, I found a window seat near the front and sat down, placing my backpack in my lap. As I looked out the window, the city's colorful buildings and large sculptures became a blur as the bus made its way through Detroit traffic. A half hour later, the bus pulled to a stop at the Ferndale junction. I hoisted my backpack—heavy with books and my riding equipment—onto my back before getting off the bus. I had ten minutes until my next bus arrived, which would drop me off five minutes from the stables. As I waited, I texted the group chat with my mom and dad to let them know that I arrived at Ferndale safely. Keeping in touch with my parents was one of the conditions of allowing me to join the show team. Twenty minutes after I got on the number twelve bus, I hopped off and began heading toward the stables. As I walked through the rich-looking North End neighborhood, I couldn't stop staring at the large houses, with their beautifully manicured lawns. The sidewalks were neat and clean, very different from the cracked and sometimes trash-strewn sidewalks near my home in the South End. A few blocks later, I saw a sign reading "North Wind Acres Equestrian Center & Farm, .25 miles." As I hiked up the winding paved driveway toward the barn, I could feel the excitement and nerves rise from the pit of my stomach. I checked my watch; it flashed 3:55 p.m. I had just enough time to change into my riding clothes, tack up my assigned horse, and be ready for the lesson to begin at 4:30 p.m.

I pulled out my cell phone to text my parents to let them know that I had arrived and was going to Ms. Julie's office. With my head down and my attention focused on sending the message, I didn't notice Ms. Julie standing outside of her now-closed office door, and I bumped into her as I rounded the corner.

"Oh, Daija! There you are! Ready for your first group lesson?"

I smiled up at Ms. Julie and nodded as I tucked my cell phone back into my backpack.

"I'm SO excited!" I proclaimed, my smile widening.

"Great. You can bring your bag with you and follow me," Ms. Julie said, leading me toward the tack room. "You'll be riding Captain," she said, stopping at a locker with CAPTAIN PHOEBUS—NORTH WIND ACRES engraved on the brass placard.

"All of Captain's brushes and tack are stored here. As his assigned rider, you'll be responsible for keeping them clean and organized." I set my backpack on the locker shelf and listened carefully as Ms. Julie explained my duties. "Go ahead and grab Captain from his paddock and get tacked up for the lesson. Lessons start at four thirty sharp, and I expect riders to be mounted and warming up at that time. I'll see you in the arena," said Ms. Julie.

Twenty minutes later, I was dressed and leading Captain into the arena, where Kayla and two other riders were already mounted and warming up their horses. I waved to Kayla, then lined Captain up next to the mounting block, put one foot in the stirrup to swing myself onto Captain's back, and felt the saddle slide toward me. I clutched it as I fell off to the side. Captain nickered as if he were laughing at me, and I heard snickering from the other riders in the ring. Feeling embarrassed, I righted the saddle and tightened Captain's girth before attempting to mount again. This time, I was able to swing a leg over and climb up onto his back. As I walked Captain out to the rail to begin warming up, I heard a familiar voice whisper to me as she rode by, "He bloats a lot, so it helps to double-check his girth so you don't slip again. It's happened to me plenty of times." I looked up to see Kayla on her pony, Hershey, walking alongside Captain and me. Her dark, wavy hair was in a loose French braid that hung down her back, almost to her belt. She flashed me a bright smile before trotting forward. As I watched her ride off, I admired her shiny, tall black boots and crisp tan breeches. I looked down at my own cheap riding tights and secondhand paddock boots and half chaps, and I suddenly felt out of place.

∽

"All right, let's walk on a loose rein and begin our cooldown!" instructed Ms. Julie after our lesson. We all brought our horses down from a trot to a walk, and I patted Captain's neck as we moved. I was tired and so was Captain. Show-team lessons were more rigorous than regular lessons, and Ms. Julie was even more tough. So it was nice to get a few compliments from her during the lesson. We cooled out for the next fifteen minutes before dismounting and heading back to the barn to untack and groom our horses. After putting Captain away in his stall, I headed up to the lounge, hoping Kayla would be there. Captain was a lesson pony, so he was stabled in the lesson barn. Hershey was stalled in the boarders' barn, so I hadn't been able to talk to Kayla all afternoon. I turned on the light in the empty lounge and sat at the table before pulling out my remaining homework.

A few minutes later, the lounge door opened and the other girl and the boy from our lesson entered, laughing and talking with each other. Feeling shy, I kept my eyes down on my homework.

"Hey, you were in our lesson," I heard the boy say. I looked up at him and nodded.

"Yes, I'm Daija," I said with a shy smile.

"Hi, Daija, I'm Anthony! I've been on the show

team since last year, when I turned eleven," he said, a crooked smile on his face. He had a head full of dark, springy curls, and his teeth were stunningly white against his skin tone that seemed equal parts white and Black. His eyes were hazel, and they crinkled when he smiled. Anthony was wearing a crisp white polo shirt and tan breeches. "This is Abby," Anthony said, gesturing to the girl he had walked in with.

Abby was strikingly pretty—her brown skin was smooth and glowing, and her locs hung in waves past her shoulders. Taller than Anthony, Abby was fit, with rich brown eyes and lips that were much fuller than mine, and in her black long-sleeve polo and black breeches, she looked like an athlete. I couldn't help but stare at her.

"Hi, Abby, nice to meet you. You looked awesome in the lesson!" I said with a smile.

"Thank you, and it's Abayomi—only my friends call me Abby," she said sharply.

Anthony rolled his eyes and chuckled. "Don't mind Abby; she's just mad because you're new and really good, maybe even as good as she is." I suddenly felt very shy again, and all I could do was smile. I stared back down at my homework and tried to concentrate on finishing my algebra while Abby and Anthony took a seat at the end of the table and resumed their conversation. I could hear them discussing spending $300 on a show coat and even more on new tack for the upcoming season. I was lucky to even be on the show team and working off my lessons, and show fees didn't cover expensive show clothes or tack. When my cell phone vibrated a few minutes later with a text from my dad saying he was in the parking lot, I was grateful for a reason to leave the lounge. I bagged my books, hoisted my backpack onto my back, and slipped out quietly.

As I climbed into the minivan, my dad greeted me with a bright smile.

"How was your first lesson, kiddo?" he asked excitedly.

"It was awesome! Ms. Julie assigned me a bay gelding named Captain. He's so cute! Ms. Julie was impressed with the way I rode, she called me out in the lesson in front of the other students. I met some of the other show-team kids, and they were all super nice." I didn't mention my interaction with Abby. I had promised my parents that letting me join the show team would be a great thing, and I didn't want to worry them.

I was glad that I had met Anthony; he seemed nice. I wasn't sure that I liked Abby, but she was such a great rider that it only made sense for me to try to be her friend.

Chapter 3
Settling In

Hi, Daija

3:31 p.m.

Hi, Grandpa! How are you?

3:32 p.m.

I'm not too bad, just dealing
with a bit of a cold. How
are you?

3:35 p.m.

I'm fine; heading to the barn now. Captain and I have been making so much progress over the last month!

3:37 p.m.

That is excellent.

3:37 p.m.

It took a few weeks for me to really figure him out; I fell off him in our first lesson. We've focused on flatwork so that we can improve our canter and our transitions. Ms. Julie has been impressed with how far we've come.

3:39 p.m.

Flatwork is the most important. It sets the foundation for all of your riding. That instructor of yours is smart.

3:41 p.m.

She really is! And she explains things so well. If I have a hard time understanding what she is talking about, Ms. Julie describes stuff differently when I need it, which is good because the other kids seem to pick things up right away.

3:43 p.m.

Well, as long as you are willing to listen and learn, you will gain all the knowledge that the other kids have, too. Keep your head in the game, kiddo. I believe in you.

3:44 p.m.

Thanks, Grandpa. I'm almost at my bus stop for the barn. I'll talk to you later. I hope your cold gets better!

3:45 p.m.

Thank you, my dear. We'll talk soon.

3:46 p.m.

It had only been a little over a month since I started as a working student at North Wind Acres, but I was already settled into my routine. When I got to the stables for show-team lessons on Friday, I began my barn chores immediately. As I fed hay to the horses, Anthony entered the barn dressed in tan breeches, an olive-green sweater, and his school shoes. Even though show-team groups rotated each week, Kayla and Anthony were in most of my lessons.

"Hey, Anthony," I called from the end of the barn aisle.

"WHAT'S UP, DAIJA!" Anthony shouted back enthusiastically. I chuckled and shook my head as I lifted two flakes of hay into the last stall, closing the door firmly behind me. Anthony was goofy and never seemed to take anything too seriously, but despite this, he was a pretty skilled rider. He could even be better than Abby, if he put in more effort.

"Have you seen Kayla?" I asked as I parked the now-empty wheelbarrow in the stall at the front of the barn. "I left school early for a dentist appointment, but I thought she'd be here by now."

Anthony shook his head no and disappeared into the tack room. I pulled my phone from my pocket and sent Kayla a text.

> Hey, are you tacking up?
>
> 4:12 p.m.

Anthony poked his head out of the tack room and said, "Kayla's name is crossed off the lesson list."

"Oh," I answered, disappointed. Riding with Kayla was great because she was always supportive and helpful, and I never felt embarrassed if I made a mistake in front of her.

My phone pinged with a text from Kayla.

No, I'm not riding tonight. I'm not feeling good.

4:13 p.m.

Aww! Okay, feel better!

4:13 p.m.

"Abby is riding in our lesson tonight instead," said Anthony, emerging from the tack room with bridle, gloves, and helmet in hand. "So it'll be us three and Justin."

My face fell as I listened to Anthony. Abby and I hadn't had any lessons together since my first, since she now had soccer practice on Wednesdays and Fridays. I felt nervous to ride in front of her— she was the best on show team, and she knew it. Even though we were both friends with Kayla and Anthony, she and I knew to stay out of each other's way. Although I had known Kayla for years, she, Abby, and Anthony had been a friend group at the barn for a long time. And Abby, who was thirteen but acted much older, made me feel like an outsider.

I made my way to the tack room to grab Captain's brushes and get him ready for our lesson. When I returned, Abby was clipping her pony, Khan, onto the middle set of crossties, behind Anthony and his pony, Ranger.

"Don't be late!" called Anthony as he unclipped Ranger from the crossties and made his way toward the arena.

"Hi, Abby," I said.

"Hello, Daija," she responded without turning to look at me.

I tried to hide the frown on my face as the two of us groomed and tacked up our horses in awkward silence. As Abby set the black-and-gold saddle pad on Khan's back, I glanced at her outfit. I admired her black breeches, black vest, and golden base-layer top and shiny, tall black boots. The colors made her skin look rich and glowy. She perfectly matched Khan's black-and-gold saddle pad and matching ear bonnet. I turned back to Captain and used my arm to brush some dust off his saddle before slipping the bit into his mouth and the bridle over his head. Khan's hoofbeats echoed off the cobblestone barn floor as Abby led him toward the arena. I gathered my braids into a loose, low ponytail before pulling on my helmet and clasping it beneath my chin. I straightened my old sweatshirt and pulled my half chaps up as high as I could to smooth out the wrinkles that had formed from them being slightly too big. I felt underdressed and sloppy compared to Abby, and even Anthony. I only owned three pairs of breeches and rode in secondhand clothes, while Abby seemed to have a new outfit whenever I saw her. Captain nickered and pawed the ground. It was as if he were trying to pull me from my negative thoughts. With each lesson, we became more and more in sync, and it felt good to ride a horse that I connected with so well.

"You're right; looks don't matter," I said to Captain as I gathered his reins in my hand and began leading him out of the barn. I kept one hand on his neck to feel his warmth as we walked. I pictured us having another great ride, and I felt my self-doubt begin to fade.

As we entered the arena, the ring felt crowded. There was a vertical jump course of twelve-inch-tall poles, crossed in the middle to make cross rails, set up. I watched Anthony, on Ranger, cantering circles at the far end of the arena; Abby and Khan doing stretches; and Justin, who had just mounted his pony, steering toward the rail. I parked Captain next to the mounting block and checked his girth one final time before climbing aboard his back. Captain took a step forward, walking off from the mounting block before I had both feet in the stirrup irons. I balanced myself and found my right stirrup quickly as I steered Captain toward the rail to begin our warm-up. A few minutes later, Ms. Julie—dressed in her signature North Wind Acres sweatshirt, tan breeches, and country boots— entered the arena and took her usual seat on the mounting block in the center of the ring.

"Today's lesson, we'll try some jumps," Ms. Julie called out. Ms. Julie had me focus on flatwork and ground poles for the past month to gain confidence on Captain, so this would be my first time jumping with him. Jumping was my favorite part of riding because nothing felt better than soaring over a jump. Captain seemed to pick up on my change in mood; I felt his energy rise beneath me. I took a deep breath to steady my nerves. Ms. Julie called us all to a halt and mapped out the course and rider order. Before I knew it, Captain and I were off, third in the rotation. I lined Captain up to go through a bounce exercise. I had already picked up the canter and was approaching the first cross rail when the booming sound of a cell phone ringtone ricocheted off the arena walls. Captain spooked and ducked out of the jump to the right, and I fell over his shoulder to the ground.

"WHOAAAAA," Ms. Julie called out to Captain as he cantered away from me. "Daija, are you all right?" she asked, catching Captain by his reins and walking toward me.

"I'm okay," I mumbled, standing and dusting the arena sand off my backside.

"Are you sure?" Ms. Julie asked, as she tilted my head upward toward her to look in my eyes. "How does your head feel?"

"Yes, ma'am, I'm fine," I said as I wiggled my fingers and toes to show her that everything felt normal. Then I felt something on my back that wasn't normal. But it was just Captain nudging me and nickering softly, almost as if to say, *Sorry that I dumped you, that noise was scary!*

"Okay, do you feel good enough to get back on and cool him out?"

Not wanting to look scared, I nodded and walked Captain over to the mounting block. I climbed back onto him, and he gave a big sigh. I patted his neck as I walked him slowly to cool him out.

"This is why cell phones are never allowed in the

ring! Anthony, you know better than to have your cell phone on you! I hope you apologize to Daija after this lesson, young man," Ms. Julie said in her stern voice. She was one of the nicest people ever, but when she had to be strict, she was scary!

Anthony gave me an apologetic look from across the arena, and I nodded his way in return. I hadn't wanted to get him into trouble. As Ms. Julie instructed everyone else to cool out on a loose rein, I exhaled deeply, happy to be done with the day's lesson. Captain walked quickly, but he was less tense beneath me. With every ride, I loved this horse a little more. It was almost like we had a secret language between us, and even though we were still figuring each other out, he had a heart of gold and took care of me even on my nervous days.

Ten minutes later, Ms. Julie's voice rang out in the arena, "Go ahead and halt and dismount, everyone.

Good job today. Anthony, you hang back—I'd like to have a word with you."

❦

"I'm sorry, Daija, I completely forgot that my phone was in my pocket!" Anthony said as he clipped Ranger onto the crossties beside me. His usually sandy-brown cheeks were bright red, and his hazel eyes were filled with regret. I didn't want him to think that I was mad at him, because I wasn't—I was more embarrassed that I couldn't control my horse and had fallen off in front of everyone, especially Abby.

Abby rolled her eyes at Anthony as she walked past us on her way to the tack room. Not wanting to make a big deal about it, I said, "It's okay, Anthony. I'm fine."

"I really am sorry—I have some of my mom's granola in my lunchbox in the lounge. You can have it as part of my apology. Why don't you come up to the lounge with us after we finish here?" said Anthony.

"Okay, sure. I'll meet you there," I said as I turned back to Captain.

Anthony and Abby finished grooming their ponies and made their way to the lounge, leaving Captain and me in the barn alone. I was grateful to have this moment with Captain. As I brushed through his mane, he craned his neck to the side and nickered softly.

"Ah, does that spot feel good?" I asked as I continued to brush his mane. Captain's head began to droop, and his lip quivered as he dozed off. I laughed quietly to myself and hugged his neck, inhaling the scent of his coat and hay. One of the things I loved most about Captain was his sweet nature. He didn't mind if I sat in his stall for an hour, since he would even lie down with me in there. I gave Captain a peppermint from my pocket before locking his stall door and making my way to meet Abby and Anthony.

As I entered the lounge, Abby and Anthony were seated at the table, talking animatedly about our lesson. Placed on the table was a bag filled with granola.

"You know, Daija," started Abby, her mouth full of granola, "Anthony fell off Ranger almost every jump lesson for a year. It got so bad his mom almost sold Ranger."

"NOT TRUE!" retorted Anthony, his cheeks turning even more red.

"*Really?*" I asked, my eyes wide with surprise.

"*Yup!* He couldn't get over a cross rail for months. A few kids test rode Ranger, but Anthony cried every time they came, so eventually his mom decided to keep him." Abby's eyes shined with amusement as Anthony tried to hide his now-crimson cheeks with his hands.

"Ranger was a gift for my older brother from my dad, no way we could sell him!" Anthony responded. I had known that Ranger used to be Anthony's brother's main mount, and when he moved up the levels, Anthony started riding Ranger. Anthony's parents weren't together anymore, but he was close with his dad, and even though he got into riding because his mom loved horses, his dad was very supportive. I wouldn't be surprised if he was the one who had convinced Anthony's mom to keep Ranger.

"Besides, you fell off Captain more than I fell off Ranger, Abby," Anthony shot back, sneering.

"Everyone falls off Captain," Abby said coolly.

As Abby and Anthony went back and forth, I couldn't help but be surprised that Abby had ridden

Captain. Abby's parents were very wealthy. One of her moms was a banker, and her other mom was a doctor. Khan was imported from Germany, so it never occurred to me that she had ridden lesson ponies before.

"When did you ride Captain?" I piped in, cutting the bickering short.

"Two years ago," said Abby. "My moms didn't want to buy anything until they were sure I'd stick with riding. When I asked to join the show team last year, they understood that I was dedicated, and that's when we bought Khan. Captain is a great horse—if you know what you're doing." Abby gave me a smile. I couldn't tell if her "if you know what you're doing" comment was a dig at me. But I was enjoying the conversation, so I relaxed a bit and shook the thoughts from my mind.

Chapter 4
Winter Break

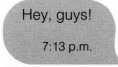

Hey, guys!

7:13 p.m.

KAYLA

Hi!

7:13 p.m.

ABBY

Hi

7:13 p.m.

ANTHONY

What's up?

7:13 p.m.

Nothing much,
drinking hot cocoa
and working on
homework. What
are you guys
doing?

7:16 p.m.

ABBY

I'm getting my hair done
for my mom's charity ball
tonight. My dress is so
pretty—the sleeves are
covered in crystals, and
the skirt is the softest
velvet ever!

I got blue-velvet heels
to wear with it, too.

7:17 p.m.

KAYLA

My mom, abuela, and I are having a girls' day today. I got a manicure, and we are heading to the mall for some shopping!

7:18 p.m.

ANTHONY

Colorado is COLD! The slopes aren't crowded, though, so that's fun.

7:18 p.m.

As my phone buzzed with more text messages, I could see our group text getting flooded with pictures of Abby's dress, Kayla's manicure, and Anthony posing in front of the mountains in Aspen. I locked my screen before shoving my cell phone into my pocket. Even though it was nice to be included in the group chat, and I was the one who had texted everybody, these pictures were a reminder of how different our lives were.

Anthony and his brother were visiting his father in Colorado for Anthony's birthday. They were staying in his family's chalet in Aspen for a weekend of skiing and snowboarding.

My family took one vacation a year. We usually drove down to Virginia to visit Grandpa Joe and Grandma Sheila, and while I loved seeing my grandparents, it was the same routine. My family didn't take ski trips, and the last time my mom and I had a girls' day was for my eighth birthday—three years ago. Instead of getting ready for a ball or going shopping, I was at home working on a school project for extra credit, while my mom was doing overtime at the hospital and my dad was working in his study downstairs.

I sighed and shoved my geography project to

the side. I didn't want to do anything responsible anymore. I opened my laptop and watched videos of top riders training and showing, since that always made me feel better. As I watched Olympic rider Jade Taylor fly over a three-foot-three-inch oxer of two sets of poles set three feet apart, I imagined myself in the big ring, soaring over the highest jumps with ease. I may not have had control over my family's situation, but as Grandpa Joe always reminded me, if I kept my head in the game, I could have control over how well I rode. I knew my friends didn't understand that I felt out of place with them sometimes, and that wasn't their fault.

My phone was still chiming with text alerts, so I pulled it from my pocket and began to respond to everyone's messages. Abby's dress was so cute, and despite our weird relationship, I told her that I thought she looked amazing. Kayla was my very best friend, so I was happy she and her mom were spending the entire day together. Anthony had been looking forward to visiting his dad for a while, and it was all he had talked about for the past few weeks. As the group chat died down and everyone focused on their activities, I turned back to Jade Taylor's ride. As I watched her finish the jump-off round in second place, I promised myself that I would keep my head focused so that I could ride the fanciest horse at the top levels, in my fancy show clothes, one day.

Chapter 5
Missing Out

"Excellent rhythm, Daija! Keep him straight to the jump!" Ms. Julie said as Captain and I flew through the course she'd set up for our private lesson. As we jumped a blue oxer and rounded the far turn, I counted strides in my head. *One, two, three, four, five—jump!* Captain and I were in perfect sync as we soared over the last jump and finished the course without knocking down any rails.

"Good boy," I whispered to Captain. He snorted,

as if pleased with himself, and we trotted a circle around Ms. Julie before coming down to a walk.

"That is the kind of decision-making I want to keep seeing from you! He kept pace, and you only got involved when needed. You keep riding like that, Daija, and you'll get your points at Woodridge next month."

I was a little nervous because Woodridge would be my first rated show since I joined the team five months ago, but I had been working extra hard to make sure Captain and I would be ready. And if Captain and I rode the way we did today, we would win a blue ribbon and five points, at least. The nights of studying two chapters instead of just one to make sure my grades stayed up, being fully focused during every lesson and practice ride, and getting all of my barn chores completed with enough time to watch other lessons was paying off.

"That was awesome!" I exclaimed. "I've never felt more in sync with him than just now."

"That's fantastic! Go ahead and cool down for ten minutes. Then you can take care of Captain."

After our cooldown, the next stop was the barn to start my chores. I was so happy, I didn't even mind that I would be feeding hay and sweeping.

As I headed to the barn, I replayed today's lesson in my head. I relived each moment—the feeling of flying during every jump, the drop in my stomach—as if Captain and I were still in the arena. I patted Captain's neck to thank him for having such a great ride. He nickered loudly as if to say, *"You're welcome."*

"DAIJAAAAA!!!!!" I heard a voice shout from behind me.

Captain and I turned to see Anthony, Abby, and Kayla walking toward us, their ponies beside them.

"Hey, guys," I said as my friends—and Abby—neared.

"How was your lesson—was your girth tight?" asked Abby with a smirk as we all continued walking.

Ignoring Abby's snarky comment, I replied, "It was amazing! Captain flew through that course and didn't knock down a single rail. It's the best we've ever ridden!"

"That's awesome, Daija!" said Kayla, smiling warmly and pulling her cap down over her ears.

"Think you're ready for Woodridge next month?" asked Anthony as he tried to yank Ranger away from a patch of green grass.

"We are ready for sure! You might need to do more work with Ranger," I said, laughing, as Anthony again yanked Ranger's head up and away from the few stalks of grass peeking through the snow.

"Well, we're going on a hack now. Come with us!" said Kayla.

Going on a hack with the gang sounded like a lot of fun! I had been so focused on preparing for Woodridge that I hadn't ridden the trails in weeks. Plus, I had already used my one practice ride for the week.

"That sounds like fun, but I have to finish barn chores now."

"Oh, come on. You can finish barn chores when we get back," Anthony countered, his voice cracking a bit as he spoke. "You're the only student to have ridden with Ms. Julie for less than a year who is allowed to hack out solo! You can't miss this!"

Anthony didn't always understand why I couldn't blow off my chores. His family was rich, and he and Abby went to one of the best schools in Michigan.

"Sorry, guys, maybe next time. I can't slack off on my chores if I want to keep riding Captain."

"That's okay, Daija, we can all ride together another day," offered Kayla, giving me one of her kindhearted smiles and a pat on my shoulder.

After a few awkwardly quiet minutes, they all filed out and only Captain and I were left. As I brushed Captain's mane, he scratched his face up and down my back before letting out a big yawn and dropping his head over my shoulder to let me slip on his halter. Captain was more than just my lesson horse; he was becoming my best friend. So that's how he knew I felt sad that I had to miss out on the hack. I wished more than anything that I owned Captain so I could ride him whenever I liked, but I knew owning a horse was not something my family could afford. I led Captain into his stall and dropped an extra carrot into his feed bin before locking his stall door.

An hour after feeding hay, sweeping the barn aisle, and starting my reading assignment on *So Far from the Bamboo Grove*, I watched Abby, Kayla, and Anthony, smiling, walk into the lounge.

"How was the hack?" I asked.

"We saw deer. You missed a fun time!" answered Abby, removing her hat. Her locs fell softly around her shoulders before she gathered them into a ponytail.

"It was a lot of fun. Hershey was really excited to be out with Khan and Ranger," said Kayla.

I smiled and excused myself to go finish my last chore of the night: filling the water buckets in each stall. Kayla offered to help me, which was sweet, but I knew I needed to be alone. Walking out, I felt a little annoyed. I was grateful to Ms. Julie for allowing me to work off the costs for being on the show team, but some days I wanted to be able to just hang out with everyone.

As I entered a stall to fill the water bucket, Kayla's pony, Hershey, nuzzled my back, and I gave him a scratch on the nose and a treat from my pocket. Kayla's mom began leasing Hershey for her after Kayla's dad died two years ago. Hershey, a dappled bay Welsh cross, had the sweetest personality of all the horses in the barn. He and Kayla were very similar; they always made you feel loved.

I slipped into Captain's stall after I had given water to the rest of the horses, and I sat in the corner, watching him as he quietly munched on his hay.

"I'm sorry I couldn't take you on a hack with your friends today. I'm so happy to be a part of the show team; I wouldn't be riding you if I wasn't." I twirled a piece of hay between my fingers as I vented. "But all I do is work. I can barely hang out for two seconds before something else needs to be done. Plus, all this working isn't even helping me pay for new clothes. I'm tired of wearing old T-shirts instead of riding shirts and these old, scuffed boots instead of shiny, new ones."

Captain made his way over to me and dropped his head right into my hands. I petted his face as I felt my frustrations growing.

"Sometimes I feel so out of place. I'm lucky that Kayla and I knew each other before I started riding. Everyone else only likes me because they have to. I'm not one of them."

Right then, I felt my phone vibrating in my pocket. As I stood from the stall floor, I pulled out my phone and read the message from my dad: Be there in 5.

"Goodbye, buddy," I whispered to Captain, hugging his neck tightly and kissing his nose, before exiting his stall. Even though he couldn't respond, I could tell he understood how I was feeling. As I turned from locking the stall door, I bumped into someone.

"Oh! Good night, Ms. Julie, I was just leaving." I hadn't noticed her enter the barn, and I wasn't sure how much of my conversation with Captain she had heard. I suddenly felt nervous.

"Good night, Daija. Great job again, today's lesson was fabulous."

"Thank you, ma'am," I said.

I turned toward the barn doors and was about to make my way to the lounge when I heard Ms. Julie's voice calling to me.

"Daija," she began, "I know that having so much responsibility at your age can be tough. I remember balancing being a working student, having a part-time job, going to school, and riding when I was younger. I was a few years older than you, and it was still hard for me. My family couldn't afford any lessons for me, but I got lucky and won a lesson package in a raffle at my elementary school. After my first ride, I was obsessed. Once those lessons ran out, I had to get creative and find a way to ride. I didn't get my first pair of paddock boots for almost a year after I started riding."

I listened to Ms. Julie, surprised that she hadn't come from a wealthy family. Looking at her and North Wind Acres, you would think the opposite.

"I stayed focused; gave every single ride my best shot; asked questions; offered to groom, ride, rehab, and work any and every horse that I could. I rode a lot of horses that weren't fancy, and I could never step foot in the show ring, but every horse that I've worked with has taught me an important lesson. The best riders are the ones who have passion for their horses and who sacrificed the most to feed that passion. Just remember that when you get frustrated."

I felt a lump in my throat. I didn't want Ms. Julie to think that I wasn't appreciative; it was just hard fitting in when I clearly didn't.

Chapter 6
First Flight

"All right, everyone, please make sure you have everything that you need for today! Helmets, boots, gloves, etcetera. Woodridge is two hours away, so there's no time to turn back—Anthony, that means BOTH boots need to be packed in your bag this time!" Ms. Julie shouted reminders and instructions as we sat on the arena bleachers. We all laughed as Anthony nodded, his face turning red.

It was the morning of the Woodridge show. The

braids I put in Captain's mane and tail looked great, and his tack trunk was packed and loaded onto the trailer. As I sat next to Kayla and Abby, I couldn't help but be nervous and excited. Woodridge was one of the bigger shows in Michigan, and there would be a lot of riders attending—which meant a lot of competition.

"Now! I know everyone is full of energy. Remember, we've practiced extensively for this. Trust yourselves, and most importantly, trust your horses." Ms. Julie clapped her hands together, signaling us all to stand.

"WHO ARE WE?" she called.

"NORTH WIND ACRES!" we chanted back, putting our hands together in a circle before breaking and cheering.

"Now let's head out!" Ms. Julie called, leading us out of the arena. As we climbed into our cars, Ms.

Julie led the caravan of show-team families down the winding driveway and toward Woodridge. My dad had to work, so it was only my mom and me making the trip.

"How are you feeling, Daija?" asked Mom as we followed behind Ms. Julie in the trailer.

"I'm nervous," I confessed. "I just want to do well."

"It's okay to be nervous; it's your first big show. But you've done such a good job preparing."

"What if I fall?"

"Everyone falls, even professionals. Do you remember when you had your ballet recital when you were eight? You practiced your routine day and night. At home, at school, walking through the grocery store—you would not stop." Mom chuckled as she reminisced. "Then the day of the recital, when it was time for your solo, you stepped to the front of the stage and did your routine perfectly. Not a missed step. Today is no different. You've practiced, and you've prepared Captain—you've got this."

My mom was right; Captain and I were ready for Woodridge. Most of my nerves were coming from wanting to prove to my parents, Ms. Julie, and everyone else that Captain and I were serious competition even if we weren't the fanciest.

A little over two hours later, we pulled onto the Woodridge show grounds. I stared in awe at how busy the place looked. Horses were being unloaded from trailers, some were being warmed up in the arenas, some were being hand-grazed, and others were being bathed. As my mom parked the car next to the North Wind Acres trailer, I climbed out and found my friends.

"I have the class schedule for the day; our first class is in an hour. Take this time to get dressed and polish your boots if you haven't already. In about half an hour, we will tack up and head to the warm-up ring," Ms. Julie instructed from the back of the trailer. Kayla and I nervously chatted as Ms. Julie continued. "The first class will be Abby, Anthony, Stacey, and Justin. The next class will be Kayla, Daija, Simone, and Aiden."

I wished Abby and Anthony good luck as I headed back to my parents' van to unload my show clothes. Anthony smiled while Abby just nodded her head and walked off. I picked up the garment bag with my hand-me-down show coat and spare show shirt from the van. I was already wearing my show shirt and tan breeches beneath a pair of black sweatpants and a hoodie. I grabbed my duffel bag and headed over to the trailer.

"Okay, buddy, we're going to ride just like we do at home," I said to Captain as I tacked him up. Captain snorted and continued to eat hay, seemingly unfazed by the busy show environment. I was glad that at least one of us was not a big ball of nerves. When I finished with Captain, I put on my navy show coat, with the North Wind Acres emblem embroidered on the sleeve. Then I zipped myself into the tall boots Ms. Julie had let me borrow. They were old, but I had spent a good amount of time cleaning and polishing them, and they looked good enough to show in. I gathered my braids in a low ponytail and tried to slip my helmet on, but my hands were unsteady. I groaned in frustration as I pulled my helmet off of my head and tried to fix my hair.

"Need some help?"

I turned to find Anthony behind me, removing his own helmet and shaking out his springy curls. Abby was standing right next to him.

"Sure," I said, with obvious frustration in my voice.

"Why don't you hold your hair, and I'll slip the helmet on," suggested Anthony.

Handing my helmet over to him, I parted my braids down the center and laid all my hair as flat as possible. Anthony lifted the helmet onto my head and tried to push it down as hard as he could.

"OW! You can't just shove it on. You have to wiggle it down," I explained.

"Sorry, I wasn't trying to hurt you. That's just what I do with mine."

"Ugh, let me do it," Abby grumbled, taking my helmet from Anthony.

I wasn't upset with Anthony. Even though he is half Black, his hair is nothing like ours. He didn't have to deal with bulky braids or long locs. A minute later, Abby and I managed to get the helmet comfortably on my head before she turned and left without saying another word. That was the nicest she had ever been to me, so I took it as my first win of the day. Hopefully, I would get one more.

"Good luck, Daija," said Anthony as I slid the reins over Captain's head. Anthony had been showing for years, so the environment didn't affect him. But I could feel myself beginning to sweat. I took a few deep breaths before gathering Captain's reins in one hand and leading him away from the trailer and toward the warm-up arena.

"*Easy, boy*," I said to Captain as I felt his energy rise beneath me. Captain was thirteen years old, so he was mature enough to understand his job but still young enough to have lots of energy and spirit. I focused on keeping him in sync with me as we did loops of walk, trot, and canter in both directions around the ring. Captain felt excited but not anxious, which helped my nerves begin to fade.

"All right, North Wind Acres students, it's time to enter the ring!" called Ms. Julie from the side of the warm-up arena. I led the North Wind Acres students out to the sidelines of the show ring, where we waited our turns to enter.

As I sat atop Captain and watched the rider before me turn into the line for the last three jumps, Ms. Julie walked over to me.

"Okay, Daija, remember to keep his pace nice and steady and to keep him straight. If you line him up properly, he'll do the rest. You've got this," Ms. Julie said, flashing me a bright smile and patting my leg.

I nodded a silent yes in return and gathered my reins. I squeezed Captain's sides gently with my calves and signaled him to walk on. As we entered the arena, I took a deep breath before beginning the course.

As I cantered Captain into position for the first jump, I counted my strides: *one, two, three—JUMP!* As Captain lifted off from beneath me and soared over the first jump, I felt my nerves finally disappear. All I could think about was how amazing Captain was doing. His jumps at home had been phenomenal, but it was almost like he knew we were at a show. We landed on the correct lead and took off like lightning through the rest of the course.

"Keep him straight! Pace yourself!" I heard Ms. Julie call out. I centered my hands, squeezed Captain's sides with my calves, and sat deep in the saddle as we rounded our final turn for the last line of jumps.

"Okay, boy, last three. Come on, we've got this."

Captain snorted in response as we flew over the first jump in our final line. We kept a steady pace and zoomed over the last two jumps—leaving every rail in place. As I brought Captain back down to a trot, I smiled so hard my face hurt, and I patted his neck enthusiastically as we exited the ring.

"EXCELLENT, DAIJA!" exclaimed Ms. Julie as she approached us. "You two looked like seasoned pros in there. I am so proud of you."

My smile was glued in place. I dismounted and walked Captain over to the horse trailer to munch on hay. There were nine more riders to go before a winner would be pinned.

"That was fabulous, Daija!" said my mom, engulfing me in a big hug. I managed a small thank-you as I removed my show coat and took a seat on the edge of the trailer, but I was having a hard time talking because I couldn't find the words to describe how incredible I felt.

Kayla and Anthony appeared behind my mom, with big smiles on their faces, but Abby came over scowling.

"That was a beautiful round, Daija!" said Kayla enthusiastically. Anthony nodded in agreement and high-fived me.

"It was okay," said Abby coolly. "You could have made that sixth jump in seven strides, but your skill level isn't there yet, so it was smart of you to do eight instead. Khan and I did it in six strides." I tried not to let Abby's comments dampen my mood.

Fifteen minutes later, I was pulling my show coat back on and mounting Captain to return to the ring to find out if we had placed. As I lined up with the other riders, I felt the nerves rush back over me. I wanted more than anything to place so that I could get the ten points I needed to qualify for Finals. As I watched the third- and second-place riders get called, I began to worry: Captain and I had one of our best rides yet, but was it enough to take the blue ribbon?

"... *and the grand champion is number twenty-seven, Daija Williams-Reed aboard Captain Phoebus.*"

My head snapped straight up as I heard my name called. I couldn't believe I had done it! I walked Captain forward, toward the show steward, and beamed as she pinned a blue ribbon to Captain's bridle. *Grand champion! Not only did Captain and I just win first place, we also scored fifteen points toward qualifying for Finals! We are ahead of the game!* As Ms. Julie and my mom rushed over to me as I exited the ring, I hugged Captain's neck hard and whispered a thank-you in his ear. After loading Captain onto the trailer, I stepped off and rounded the open door to find Abby standing with Kayla.

"I'll see you guys back at the barn!" I said brightly.

"Sure! Congrats again on the win, Daija!" said Kayla, reaching out to hug me.

"Thanks! I'm just glad the judges thought that those eight strides were worth it," I said smartly. I looked directly at Abby, gave her my biggest smile, and clutched my blue ribbon tightly.

～

"All right, everyone, let's work on transitions and timing today!" shouted Ms. Julie from the center of the arena. It was two days after the Woodridge competition, and Ms. Julie only gave us one day of rest before lessons resumed. I was feeling particularly confident after my win with Captain and was excited to show off our progress some more in our group lesson.

As we lined up to begin the exercise Ms. Julie had laid out for us, I noticed Abby and Khan were having an unusually hard time in the arena. Khan was stiff, and Abby's timing was all off. I could see the frustration on Abby's face as she and Khan cantered by. *I'll give her some pointers after the lesson*, I thought to myself.

Twenty minutes after our lesson had ended and I finished my chores, I made my way to the lounge, where I found Abby sitting at the table doing homework.

"Hey, Abby," I said, taking a seat next to her. "Tough lesson tonight?"

Shrugging, Abby responded, "We had an off day." Abby didn't look as unbothered as she was trying to act.

"I noticed you seemed pretty tense today, and maybe that is why Khan was so stiff. You should try relaxing into the saddle more and keeping your hands firmly in front of you with your wrists relaxed."

"Thanks, but it was just an off day. It happens sometimes. We'll be fine for our next lesson."

"I bet you will be—if you remember to stay relaxed and sit deeper in the saddle. That's how Captain and I won grand champion at Woodridge."

Abby turned toward me, a slight glare on her face as she packed her work into her bag. "Khan and I will be fine, Daija. I'm going to wait for my mom by the barn."

I watched as Abby walked off in a huff. I couldn't understand why she wouldn't listen to my advice. A few minutes later, I was climbing into the back seat of my dad's car with all my stuff as we headed toward home. I pulled out my cell phone to text Kayla and tell her what happened.

Hey! Did you hear about Abby's lesson?

6:35 p.m.

Yes, she texted me. She's pretty upset.

6:42 p.m.

She was so out of tune today! She overrode every fence, and she kept lighting Khan up. I tried to tell her she needs to work on her transition cues, but she didn't want to listen to me.

6:43 p.m.

You'd think she'd take my advice since I did win Woodridge, after all. BTW, your cues could use some work, too, Kayla.

6:45 p.m.

Ms. Julie reminds us what we have to work on in every lesson. No one asked you to do it, too. I'm going to finish my homework. I'll see you in class tomorrow.

6:49 p.m.

I rolled my eyes as I locked my phone screen. I'm not sure why everyone was getting upset with me for offering them advice.

"We're home, kiddo," said my dad as he pulled into our driveway. I climbed out of the van and made my way into the house. My dad followed behind me saying, "Chores before din—"

"Chores before dinner, I know," I said without turning toward him and continuing to make my way to my room.

Chapter 7
Winds of Change

As the spring weather creeped in, my friends came to the barn more frequently, and that made working a lot more fun. Instead of using my one practice ride per week to train, I decided Captain and I had earned some time to hang out with the gang. After our win at Woodridge last month, I figured Captain and I didn't need as much practice. Our next show wasn't for another month, so we had plenty of time to get ready.

As Kayla, Anthony, and I made our way to the lounge to hang out after school, Ms. Julie pulled me aside.

"Did you hay and water the back barn, Daija?"

"Not yet, ma'am."

"Putting out the hay and water is supposed to be done by six, Daija. I've noticed it hasn't been getting done on time. Can you please go take care of it now?"

I watched and sighed as my friends went to the lounge without me.

"You were doing a fantastic job balancing your barn chores, schoolwork, and riding schedule when you first joined the team, Daija, but if things are becoming overwhelming, please let me know so that I can help you restructure your schedule."

"No need to restructure anything, ma'am. I understand how important my chores are."

"Good. When was the last time you had a practice

ride on Captain? I haven't seen you ride outside of lessons these past few weeks."

Thinking quickly, I said, "I was going to ride Captain today and work on transitions and timing."

"All right, good. I'll be in my office if you need any help."

I smiled and nodded at Ms. Julie before turning toward the barn.

"Hey, Daija, you coming?" Anthony shouted from across the driveway.

"I'll catch up with you guys later. I have to do my stupid chores."

"You're going to miss seeing the movie I made with my friends at school!"

"I'm sorry!" I replied. I knew Ms. Julie would be keeping an eye out to see me ride, so I turned and ran toward the barn. As I entered, the horses all nickered excitedly.

"Yeah, yeah, it's snack time," I groaned as I loaded the wheelbarrow with hay. *I am so sick of being the poor kid that has to work to ride here.*

❧

"Hey, Daija, Abby and I were texting and planning to go downtown tomorrow after school—want to come?" asked Anthony, after I finally made it to the lounge.

"Yes, definitely!" I answered enthusiastically.

I hadn't hung out with Anthony outside of the barn before, so I jumped at the opportunity.

"Don't you have to work on Fridays?" asked Kayla.

"I'll just work another day," I said matter-of-factly.

"Will your parents let you go?" asked Kayla.

"Oh yeah, they'll be cool with it." Truth is, I knew my parents wouldn't let me go, so I'd probably have to lie to them, but I didn't know if I would get this opportunity again anytime soon.

"Are you sure?" asked Kayla, shooting me a concerned glance. "I'll be here to ride Hershey tomorrow, and we could hang out."

I brushed her off and responded with a firm "I'm sure" before turning to Anthony. "What did you guys want to do downtown?"

"Abby said she needs new riding clothes, and I want some new boots, so we're probably going to go to the new Dover that just opened in downtown."

I nodded enthusiastically, but I felt dread in my stomach. Dover was one of the best equine retailers in the country, which meant that everything in the store was *expensive*. I only had about twenty-five dollars that I had saved from my allowance.

"I've been meaning to get some new riding shirts," I added.

"Okay, cool! Want to meet here at the barn, and we can call a car service?"

I couldn't leave from the barn; if Ms. Julie saw me, I'd have to work.

"How about we take the bus? We can meet at Lafayette Park since it's between our two schools. It'll be fun!"

"I haven't taken the bus or the train in forever! Let's do it. I'll let Abby know," added Anthony enthusiastically.

I nodded in agreement, trying to hide my excitement. Things between Abby and me were slightly better, but I knew I could get her to be my friend during this trip. I ignored Kayla's disapproving looks as I thought about my game plan. I would call Ms. Julie tomorrow after school and tell her that I didn't feel good and then I would head downtown to Dover. As long as I made it to the barn by the time Dad arrived to pick me up, and avoided seeing Ms. Julie, no one would know I had skipped out on my lesson. Besides, skipping one lesson wasn't the end of the world.

~

As I gathered my books and bag to leave school the next day, my phone dinged with a text message from Kayla.

Hey, Ms. Julie is looking for you. Maybe you should just come to your lesson instead of going to Dover. I can help you with chores after I ride, and we can hang out, just the two of us.

2:32 p.m.

Thanks for the heads-up! Don't say anything to her. We can hang out another day.

2:35 p.m.

Sure . . .

2:37 p.m.

I ducked into a stall in the girls' bathroom and dialed Ms. Julie's cell number.

Don't pick up, don't pick up, I pleaded in my head as the phone rang. I breathed a sigh of relief as I listened to Ms. Julie's prerecorded voicemail. I left a quick message, keeping my voice low so I sounded believable.

"Hi, Ms. Julie, it's Daija. I have a really bad stomachache, and I don't feel well enough to ride. I will reschedule my lesson with you for another day. Thank you."

I pressed the "end call" button on my phone screen and made my way out of the school bathroom and toward the bus stop. Fifteen minutes later, I stepped off the bus at Lafayette Park and spotted

Abby and Anthony sitting on a bench near the entrance.

"Hi, guys! The next bus should be coming in two minutes," I said as I approached them. It felt funny seeing Abby and Anthony dressed in their street clothes, which were even nicer than what they wore normally. Abby and Anthony looked so out of place as we rode the bus and maneuvered through the train station. Taking public transit was just as easy as tying my shoelaces, so I led them through the station with confidence. Abby even told me I was cool for knowing how to get around the city by myself! Forty minutes later, we exited the train station, talking and laughing as we walked down Broadway Avenue.

Entering Dover was like entering an entirely different world. Beautiful leather halters, bridles, and saddles hung on display in front of the walls.

Shadbellies, show coats, and high-end breeches were modeled on mannequins in the windows.

"Daija! We're going to try things on," called Abby. Her hands were already piled high with clothes. "Aren't you going to try anything?

"Sure," I said as I made my way over to the apparel section. I carefully thumbed through racks of breeches, making sure not to mess up anything, before a beautiful pair caught my eye. They had crystal detailing at the pockets, traditional leather knee patches, and were the perfect shade of tan.

"I think I'll try these on," I said out loud, more to myself than to Abby. I grabbed a black sweater with plaid elbow patches from the rack next to the breeches and turned toward the dressing room.

A few minutes later, I stepped out to show Abby and Anthony my outfit.

"You look awesome!" exclaimed Anthony, his

eyes wide with surprise as I emerged.

"You do! You look like a real rider," added Abby enthusiastically.

I turned to look at myself in the full-length mirror. It was true, I did look like a serious rider. I smiled outwardly, happy with the version of myself looking back at me in the mirror, but inside, I couldn't stop thinking about Abby's comment. I don't even think she meant to be mean. But she was right; in my regular, old T-shirts and riding tights, I didn't look like a "real rider." I stared at myself a bit longer as Abby and Anthony disappeared into their dressing rooms to try on more clothes. As I stood there, I turned the price tags over and over in my hands, trying to decide if I should look at what the breeches and sweater cost. As I finally peeked at the tag for the breeches, the $209.99 that stared back at me was more than I had anticipated. Abby suddenly appeared behind me and noticed the shocked look on my face.

"I could totally buy those for you, you know."

"Oh, no thanks," I answered, embarrassed.

"Honestly, it's no problem. You do look really great in that outfit."

Abby's offer didn't sound snarky, but I couldn't let her buy me an outfit worth over $300. I didn't want to feel like a charity case; plus, my parents would wonder where I got them from.

"That's okay, my parents are supposed to take me shopping for new riding gear for winning Woodridge," I lied as I entered the fitting room to change back into my regular clothes. I couldn't see Abby's face from behind the door, and I wasn't sure if she believed me, but I tried to sound as convincing as possible. I pulled my phone from my pocket and checked the time: 5:07 p.m. I only had about an hour and a half to make it back to the barn before my dad would be there to pick me up.

"Hey, guys, I think we should head back soon! We can grab food on our way," I shouted from inside the fitting room.

"Sounds good!" I heard Anthony say.

I quickly but carefully put the sweater and breeches back on their hangers. As I followed Abby and Anthony to the register, I returned the items to their spot on the rack.

"Not getting anything, Daija?" asked Anthony as the sales associate scanned through his pile of items.

"Not today. I'm going to come back with my parents. I just wanted to check out what they had so that I know what I want," I answered, avoiding eye contact with my friends as they paid for their items.

While Anthony and Abby swapped jokes and munched on fries as we walked to the train station,

I kept checking my phone. It was 5:36 p.m. when we made it to the subway platform. I was starting to panic, until I saw the subway lights illuminate the tunnel six minutes later.

As I boarded the bus at Lafayette Park thirty-eight minutes after that, I waved goodbye to Abby and Anthony, who were taking a car service home. I had just enough time to make it to the barn before my dad would be there. As I ran to the front gate of the barn, my phone vibrated with a text message from my dad: I'm here.

I climbed into the car, and my dad greeted me with his usual "Hey, kiddo." I sank back into my seat and tried to quietly catch my breath. I couldn't believe I'd gotten away with it! As we headed toward home, my phone buzzed with a text message. I opened it and saw a text from Abby that read: Had a blast today! I sent a quick reply saying Me too ☺

before locking my phone and settling back in my seat.

⤚

"Hi, Grandpa," I said, and waved, after I'd hit the green "answer" button on my phone.

"There's my little cowgirl!" said Grandpa Joe. "How was your lesson today?" Grandpa Joe's face filled my phone screen, but he looked different. His cheeks were much slimmer, and his gray hair seemed grayer than ever before. For the first time, I noticed how deep the wrinkles were around the corners of his eyes. Something in my stomach fluttered, but I pushed the worry out of my mind.

"It was great," I replied, and squirmed in my desk chair. I felt a twinge of guilt about lying to Grandpa Joe. He was the reason I loved horses, and he'd even gotten me my first lesson package; I did not want to disappoint him.

"When is your next show?"

"I have a schooling show at the end of this month, and then we show at Fieldstone next month."

If Captain and I could earn fifteen points at our next rated show, we would qualify for pony Finals. To qualify for Finals with only two shows was almost impossible, but I wanted to accomplish that and wow everyone.

"Excellent," said Grandpa Joe. "Well, I know you can do it. Focus on the things you need to tighten up before the show, and remember to always trust your horse."

As I ended my call with Grandpa Joe, I jumped right into the conversation Anthony had started in our group chat. I sat on my bed and ignored my unfinished homework that was waiting on my desk.

Chapter 8
Falling Hard

As Captain and I entered the arena, Abby, Kayla, Anthony, and a few other show-team students sat in the bleachers watching the lesson. Ms. Julie took her seat on the mounting block and watched as I warmed Captain up. Today's flatwork lesson felt a bit boring compared to how we rode at Woodridge two months ago, so I was moving on autopilot.

"All right, if he feels soft and supple, let's go ahead and pick up our canter, Daija."

I slid my outside leg back behind the girth and massaged my outside rein. I squeezed Captain's sides firmly and urged him forward, ignoring how tense he felt. Captain picked up the canter but on the wrong lead. As he surged forward, strong and unbalanced in my hands, I struggled to bring him back down to a trot. I tried again, and again he picked up the wrong lead.

"Bring him to a walk for a minute, Daija," instructed Ms. Julie. I could feel myself getting frustrated.

The next hour was spent working on making my aids as clear as possible. Our ride ended better than it had started, but not by much.

"We've got some things to work on before our schooling show that's less than two weeks away, Daija. Missing those practice rides is starting to show."

I scowled as I dismounted and led Captain out of the arena. Why did I need a practice ride *every* week if Captain and I were good enough to win grand champion at our first rated show? As we walked back to the barn, Captain nudged me in my back.

"NO!" I said to him sharply. He made me look like I couldn't ride in front of Ms. Julie and in front of my friends. I was mad at him, and I wanted him to know it.

As I slipped Captain's halter over his head and clipped him to the crossties, Kayla appeared in the doorway.

"Tough lesson tonight, huh?" Kayla asked, sitting on a square bale of hay.

"Captain was being a total brat! He wouldn't listen to me at all," I complained as I removed Captain's tack.

"I'm not so sure it was Captain not listening; you didn't ride as cleanly as you usually do."

I could feel myself glaring as I removed Captain's saddle. Our lesson wasn't great from start to finish, and I knew that, but I refused to let Kayla put all the blame on me.

"I rode the same way I always do," I shot back.

"We both know you didn't," Kayla said calmly. "I love spending time with you, but I don't think hacking out with us and skipping practice is good for you or Captain."

"How about you worry about your own riding?" I shouted after her. "You and Hershey didn't even place at Woodridge."

"You know what, Daija," said Kayla, stopping and turning back to me, her face red with anger. "Hershey and I might not have placed, but at least I'm not a lazy jerk who blames everyone else for her problems." Before I could respond, Kayla stormed out of the barn.

∽

"How was your lesson today?" asked my dad as I climbed into the back seat of our family van. Both he and my mom were in the car.

"It was great!" I lied. If my parents found out that I was wasting my practice rides goofing off with my friends, they would ground me or possibly even make me quit the show team.

"That's fantastic. Are you and Captain shooting for another blue ribbon?" asked my mom.

I smiled and nodded, ignoring the pang of worry I felt in my stomach. If Captain and I kept having rides like we did today, there would be no blue ribbons in our future.

My mind had other things to worry about than my parents' conversation in the car, but I did hear them mention Virginia, and I hoped everything was fine with Grandpa Joe.

⤳

The morning of the schooling show, Mom and I stood in the familiar North Wind Acres lounge. I let out a frustrated groan as I attempted to button my show shirt for the third time. I was more nervous for a schooling show at our home barn than I was at Woodridge.

"No need to be nervous, Daija," said my mom, moving my hands from my shirt and buttoning it for me herself. "You've prepared for this schooling show, and after Woodridge, this is just another practice."

I took a breath and smiled as she handed me my riding gloves and crop.

"You'll do fantastic, Daija—I know how hard you've been working." Mom bent down and gave me a hug and kiss on the cheek. I wasn't sure why, but something didn't feel great about the day. I literally tried to shake off the feeling and made my way to the barn to bridle Captain.

I hugged Captain's neck and whispered a soft "good boy" in his ear before slipping the reins over his head and clasping the buckles on his bridle. As I led Captain to the arena, I lined up behind the other students and ponies entering the show. Ms. Julie's voice crackled over the loudspeaker as she announced our class.

"Whoa," I said softly as I put my foot in the stirrup before swinging the other leg over Captain's back. Captain stood motionless as I mounted. I gave him a quick pat on the neck before giving his sides a light squeeze with my calves and walking him toward the rail. As we warmed up with the other riders, Captain felt energetic beneath me. I sat tall in the saddle as we transitioned into the canter.

"Riders, warm-up time is over. Let's exit the arena, please. Our first rider will be Stephanie Grossman riding Balou. Daija Williams-Reed, please queue for the next ride." I walked Captain over to the waiting area. I watched as Stephanie and Balou gracefully glided across the arena and over every jump. She attempted to take the sharp turn after the sixth fence, but she wasn't quick enough, so Balou broke from the canter to the trot, and she had to make a full circle before jumping the last line of fences. As Stephanie's time of ninety-seven seconds flashed on the clock, I saw the disappointment on her face.

"We can do better," I whispered to Captain. I focused on the first jump as I asked for the canter. Captain and I were off! We were moving fast, but every step of our ride was a fight. I focused all my attention on each jump and setting up Captain correctly. I could feel him getting tired beneath me—we hadn't jumped a full course at this speed since Woodridge, and I was regretting not taking full advantage of my practice rides.

As Captain and I readied ourselves for the sixth jump, I could tell we were approaching it way too fast and unbalanced, but I didn't stop us. Right before our takeoff, Captain ducked out of the jump and moved to the left. I flew over his shoulder and crashed into the jump poles.

The families in the audience let out a collective gasp as I rolled over onto my back. I sat up and shook my head before climbing to my feet. Nothing felt broken or out of place. I could feel my left thigh throbbing, but I could still walk. I scanned the arena to see if Captain was running around loose, but he had stopped near the arena gate, where Kayla was standing, holding his reins. I could feel my face getting hot with embarrassment as Ms. Julie rushed over to me, followed closely by my mom.

"Oh my goodness, Daija, how do you feel?"

"Fine," I said softly.

"How is your head? Move your arms and legs for me."

I moved my arms in a circle and marched in place to show everyone I was fine.

"Good. Go ahead and untack, and put Captain away. When you're finished, meet me in my office."

I nodded my head yes before walking toward Kayla and Captain.

"Are you okay?" asked Kayla, a worried expression on her face.

"I'm fine," I said, giving her a small smile.

"Are you sure? That looked really bad."

"It wasn't that bad," I said, scowling a bit as she handed Captain's reins to me. "I'm fine."

"Fine, I don't know why I even bothered to ask,"

Kayla said, before stepping to the side to let Captain and me exit the barn.

I took my time untacking and grooming. Twenty minutes later, I locked Captain in his stall and made my way over to Ms. Julie's office. I could feel the oatmeal I had for breakfast sinking to the bottom of my stomach as I approached the office door. I took a deep breath and knocked. The door swung open, and Ms. Julie and my mother sat opposite each other.

"Have a seat, Daija," said Ms. Julie.

My heart was thumping as I slid into the empty chair next to my mother. I sat on my hands so I wouldn't pick at my fingers.

"First, how are you feeling? Do you still feel okay?"

"Yes, ma'am, I feel fine. I'm kind of embarrassed."

"Well, this is why we practice our emergency

dismounts and how to fall safely. So I am glad that you are okay." Ms. Julie sighed before continuing. "Now, while falling is a part of the sport, I've noticed a lack of focus from you these past few weeks. You haven't been completing your barn chores, your care of Captain has declined, and you've even canceled a lesson."

I heard my mother inhale sharply, and I was terrified to look at her.

"When did you cancel the lesson, Daija?" asked my mom.

"Umm—" I paused.

"Look at me when I am speaking to you," my mother said sternly.

I turned in my chair to face her.

"A few Fridays ago. I got invited to go downtown with some of the kids, and I really wanted to go."

I saw the disappointment and frustration in my

mother's eyes. "So you felt that lying was the right thing to do? Daija, your father and I trusted you to keep your word and to perform to the best of your ability."

A soft "I'm sorry" was all that I could manage.

"Ms. Julie gave you an incredible opportunity because she believes in you," Mom continued. "You have an entire team of people rallying behind you because they trust you are capable of great things. Lying, sneaking off, and not doing your part is not the way to thank them for helping you to do something that you love."

I felt my eyes well up with tears.

"I know what I did was wrong, but I just wanted to fit in. My friends don't have to work here. They get to ride whenever they want, and they can hang out after."

"Daija, I understand we may not be as wealthy

as the other families here. However, that does not give you the right to say you'll do something and then decide not to."

Ms. Julie turned toward me and said, "Daija, I believe in your talent and that you can be a fantastic rider. I wouldn't have extended this opportunity to you if I thought otherwise. However, I do not think you are ready to show at Fieldstone next week." My heart sank as Ms. Julie continued. "I think a few more weeks of practice would be beneficial. There will still be two more shows this season that you can enter to earn enough points to qualify for Finals. There is a lot of work to be done, however, to make it possible."

I felt a tear slide down my cheek when I realized that I might have let a chance at Finals slip through my fingers. As my mother thanked Ms. Julie and rose to gather her coat, I followed her quickly out of the office and into the car. That was the most uncomfortably silent ride home I had ever experienced.

A few hours later, I heard the back door close firmly: *Dad is home.* I finished emptying the cat's litter box before retreating to my room to finish my homework. My palms started sweating when I heard a knock at my door.

"Daija! Open this door now," my dad's stern voice called from outside my bedroom. I opened the door, and my parents filed in. I took a seat on my bed and prepared myself for the worst. It felt like forever before someone spoke.

"Your mother and I talked, Daija," began my dad. "We are incredibly concerned with the choices you've been making lately. You've given us reason not to trust you, and that is the worst part about all this."

Dad went on, "Considering you have shown us

that riding is not your top priority, your mother and I planned on pulling you from the show team." I felt the tears well up in my eyes again.

"However, since Ms. Julie has already invested her time and resources into giving you a successful show season, it wouldn't be fair to her to remove you from the team. We will let you finish the season, but you will have new rules to follow."

I sat on my hands to keep from wriggling with excitement—I could still ride!

"While you recover from your fall, you will come straight home after school. You will complete all of your chores and have no cell phone or laptop access for the next three weeks."

My face fell as I listened to my parents rattle off the rules. No cell phone for three weeks? How would I talk to my friends?

"If you step out of line again, riding is finished.

Do you understand, Daija? You have one more chance to prove that you can follow the rules and handle the responsibilities that come with riding. We won't have this conversation again. Understood?"

"Yes, sir," I said, before handing my cell and laptop over to my father's outstretched hands, and watching my parents leave. "If you need these for homework, ask either me or your mother, and we will supervise your use."

No cell phone, no laptop, and so many people disappointed in me. For the first time, I questioned if my friendship with the barn kids was worth all this.

Chapter 9
Back to Basics

"Daija! You have five minutes to be in the car, or we are leaving without you!" my mom yelled up the stairs. "Make sure you have all of your homework with you."

I grabbed a pair of socks from my drawer before slipping on my pink cowboy boots. My parents had pulled me from school early to spend a few days at my grandparents' farm in Stony Creek, Virginia.

"Coming!" I called from my room as I frantically

stuffed my books into my backpack. I grabbed a sweatshirt and my cowboy hat from my closet before racing down the stairs and out to the car, where my dad was already in the driver's seat, buckled up and waiting. A few minutes later, my mom took her place in the front passenger seat and shut the door to our forest-green minivan. As our car pulled off toward the highway, my heart filled with anticipation.

I used to spend my summer vacations on the farm, but we hadn't been back to visit in two years. I was always excited to spend time with my grandparents, and with things still tense around our house, I was looking forward to seeing them even more. My grandpa used to give me endless pony rides on his old mare, and I couldn't wait to show him how much my riding had improved! That's if Mom and Dad would even let me near a horse after what happened last week.

"I'm glad we found some days to take this trip," my mom said to my dad. "I really need to see how bad it is." My ears perked up—what was so bad? The familiar pang of worry shot through my stomach as my dad pulled onto the highway.

Five hours later, our van rolled up the gravel driveway toward the familiar WILLIAMS FARM sign that was now being illuminated by the stunning pink sunset. As my dad stopped the car, my grandparents emerged from the house's front door. Grandpa Joe stood much taller than Grandma Sheila, his face shaded by his straw hat, but his bright white smile was still shining through. Grandma Sheila had her silver curls slicked back into a neat bun and wore a long dress with a white wrap around her shoulders. She waved frantically as I jumped out of the car and raced across the lawn to hug her.

"Look at how tall you are!" exclaimed my grandma as she folded me into her arms. "Soon you'll be taller than me!" After a week of having my friends, parents, and Ms. Julie being so upset with me, a warm hug from my grandma Sheila was exactly what I needed. After saying our hellos, we all went into the house, and I could smell, and almost taste, Grandma Sheila's home cooking.

"I've got baked macaroni resting on the stove; chicken, greens, and cornbread are warming in the oven. You all go put your bags in your rooms and wash up while I set the table so we can sit down to eat." I took the stairs two at a time. Ten minutes later, we were all seated around the table as Grandma Sheila piled our plates high. After I sat down and we said grace, I dug into my macaroni and cornbread.

"We're excited to have you all here," said

Grandpa Joe, clapping his hands enthusiastically. "The weather is supposed to be nice this weekend, so we'll have some fun."

"We're happy to be here, Dad," my mom said. "Daija especially couldn't wait."

"Hey, Daija, how would you like to help me with the cows tomorrow, and we can take the horses out for a short ride after?"

Riding with Grandpa Joe was the reason I loved horses in the first place. He would hoist me up in the saddle with him on his old mare, Felicity, and we would go for a walk around the farm. He'd always tell me I belonged in the saddle and never let me visit without taking me for a ride.

Since my mouth was filled with cornbread, all I could do was look at my parents with pleading eyes; I knew better than to try to speak with my mouth full. They said it was okay, and Grandpa

Joe gave me a wink before taking a bite out of his chicken.

⌒

The brightest sunbeams I had ever seen woke me up the next morning. As I peered through my bedroom window, I could see my dad and Grandpa Joe loading hay into the back of his truck. I took a shower before joining them outside.

"Nice hat you've got there, kiddo," said Grandpa Joe, tapping the top of my cowboy hat.

I gave Grandpa Joe a small smile. I was happy to be on the farm, but the sting of the schooling show and missing Fieldstone was still on my mind.

"I figured we could take the old girls out for a trail ride today. How does that sound?"

"Sure," I said.

"Atta girl," he said in his Southern twang. "Let's

finish feeding these cows and then saddle up!"

Grandpa Joe, my dad, and I got to work making mash for the cows and filling the feed troughs and water troughs. The sun began to beat down on us just as we finished.

"Okay, Joe, I'm going to head up to the house," Dad said as we finished feeding the cows. "You two have fun on your trail ride!"

～

Despite how tiny he seemed to have gotten, Grandpa Joe lifted me with ease and plopped me onto Roxy's back before mounting Felicity.

"Let's roll out!" Grandpa Joe called in his gruff cowboy voice. I laughed as the horses walked off slowly, and Grandpa Joe began singing one of his old western songs. As we made our way toward the trail, Grandpa Joe asked, "How's your riding going?"

"It's fine."

"Just fine? Come on, tell me what's going on. How was the schooling show?"

"It was okay. I fell, but I'm fine and so is Captain." I hoped my answer would be enough, but I could tell Grandpa Joe wasn't taking the hint that I didn't want to talk about it.

"Hmm, well, falling is part of the sport," he said thoughtfully. "So what happened?"

"Captain wasn't very focused, and he didn't turn into the last line properly."

"Did you set him up to turn properly?"

"Yes," I said defensively.

"Now, Daija, what have I always taught you?"

"We never blame the horse; it's always rider error."

"Exactly."

I rolled my eyes as I scratched Roxy's mane.

Grandpa Joe knew me well, and he could sense when I wasn't telling the entire truth.

"Maybe I didn't set him up perfectly, but he also wasn't listening to me. He was super energetic from the moment I got on, and I knew it wasn't going to be our best ride."

"Your horse having energy is not the issue. Did you lose focus, Daija?"

I got quiet. Grandpa Joe continued, "Your mother told me that you've seemed to be less focused these past few weeks, Daija—skipping lessons, lying, not practicing as hard as you should be. What's going on?"

"I just wanted to hang out with my friends. Is that so wrong? It's hard to be the 'poor kid' at the barn. I just wanted to fit in. I don't always want to have to work. I know that I should've practiced harder, and I know I shouldn't lie, but sometimes I wish I could have my own horse, ride when I want to, and not have to be there an hour early or an hour after my lesson just to afford it."

"Do you know, Daija, money isn't everything? Money doesn't equal talent. You have natural abilities. You may have to sacrifice some things to be the best, but I know you can do it."

I tried, but I couldn't stop myself from crying.

"Oh, Daija," Grandpa Joe said as we stopped riding. "I know it's hard to balance responsibility with fun, but if anyone can figure it out, it's you. We all mess up and lose our way sometimes, but we can always get better."

One thing I loved about Grandpa Joe was that he always made me feel like I could fix things when I made a mistake, and he never loved me any less.

About half an hour later, Grandpa Joe and I

turned around the creek and headed back home. The sun was shining brightly as we walked across the field toward the barn, and Grandpa Joe instructed me to wait for him in his office while he put the horses back in the paddock.

While I looked for the light switch in the dusty office, he entered and pulled out a photo from one of the file cabinets in the corner. Grandpa Joe wiped off the frame and handed it to me. There was a man pumping a beautiful chestnut horse over a giant oxer.

"Who is this?" I asked, tilting the frame to get a better look at the photo. Before Grandpa Joe could answer, I exclaimed, "THAT'S YOU!"

"Do you recognize that horse?" he asked.

I squinted and realized that the small white star on the horse's head looked familiar.

"Is that Roxy?" I asked in disbelief.

Grandpa Joe smiled and said, "That is Roxy's mom." Roxy and her mom looked almost identical, although Roxy was much thicker, and her forehead had grayed out a lot in her old age. But Grandpa Joe's forehead had tons more lines now than it did in the picture.

"That was my very last grand prix. I won first place against forty other riders and was offered a shot to ride in the Olympics. Your grandma was pregnant with your mom, and riding professionally didn't pay the bills, so I gave it up to take care of my family. But riding is in your blood, Daija."

I stared at Grandpa Joe in awe. I couldn't believe he had ridden professionally! I always thought that he rode for fun. Then he pulled out something else from his cabinet.

"This is my grand prix first-place ribbon. I want you to hold on to this, and whenever you get frustrated, insecure, or worried, I want you to remember that you are a champion."

I took the old ribbon and turned it over in my hands. It was faded, and the gold lettering that said "first place" had lost its shimmer, but it was the most beautiful blue ribbon I had ever seen. I held it gently and looked up at Grandpa Joe.

"Our mistakes do not define us, Daija. If you want to get back out there and continue to show, I will help you, but what I need from you is to promise that you will give it your all. I know you're missing out on a show right now, but we can practice and get you ready for the next one. I have faith in you, Daija, but I need you to have faith in yourself. Deal?"

My grandpa Joe was a strong man, but as I looked at him in that moment, he didn't look so strong. I noticed how much weight he had lost and how his usually bright brown eyes were a little cloudy. I wanted nothing more than to win a blue ribbon on Captain to show Grandpa Joe that he was right about me.

"Deal!" I exclaimed, high-fiving him.

∽

"Rise and shine, cowgirl! Time to get to training; meet me in the barn!"

I heard Grandpa Joe's voice echo from the other side of my bedroom door. I opened my eyes and jumped out of bed excitedly. I rushed to the bathroom to brush my teeth before changing into my riding clothes and heading downstairs.

As I approached the back door, I heard Grandma Sheila's voice from around the corner say, "AHT-AHT, no riding on an empty stomach, young lady! Breakfast is in the oven; fruit is in the fridge."

Even at seven in the morning, Grandma Sheila

had an entire spread prepared. I grabbed an apple and gave Grandma Sheila a kiss on the cheek before heading out the back door and running down to the barn.

Grandpa Joe put Felicity and I through the course he'd set up—flatwork and ground poles— many times before he set up a few jumps. I could feel my breath catch in my throat when Grandpa Joe told us to go, but I thought about my family, Captain, and all the people who were rooting for me. I squeezed Felicity's sides with my calves and picked up a canter. As we rounded the first turn, I sat up, grabbed Felicity's mane, and exhaled as she beautifully soared over the first jump. A few more jumps later, and I was feeling great! I couldn't wait to practice these with Captain.

"You did wonderful, Daija!" Grandpa Joe said before pausing to let out a deep, scratchy cough. "You know, you have so many people rooting for you, and it's important to cherish them and apologize when you're wrong."

"Thank you, Grandpa," I said softly. "I don't think I realized how hard it would be to balance everything and to make everyone proud."

"Everyone is already proud of you, Daija, but maintaining that pride can be tricky. It's important to know when to ask for help. I won't always be here. So if you're overwhelmed, worried, or afraid, you can always talk to your mom and dad, Grandma Sheila, your friends, and your trainer. You never have to tackle anything alone."

⌒

As I wrapped my braids in my bonnet later that night, I was feeling much better. I had apologized to my mom and dad after my lesson, and I decided that a piece of Grandma Sheila's pumpkin pie and a glass of milk was the perfect reward. As I made my way past the living room toward the kitchen, I overheard my mom and Grandma Sheila talking quietly.

"Why didn't he tell me sooner?" I heard my mom say. Her voice sounded as if she was crying.

"You know your father. He always acts as if nothing is wrong. The doctors say there isn't more that can be done."

I froze as I realized they were talking about Grandpa Joe! It sounded like Grandpa Joe was sicker than he let on. Is this why he was talking about not being around? A wave of worry and sadness washed over me, erasing my appetite. I sneaked silently back upstairs to my room. I climbed into bed with Grandpa Joe's blue ribbon tucked under my pillow and pulled the covers tightly under my chin as I tried not to think about this news.

Chapter 10
Making Amends

As I walked up the winding driveway toward the stables, I pulled out my cell phone and texted my parents in our group chat that I had made it safely. My family had returned from our visit to my grandparents a week ago, and I was allowed to resume riding today, so I finally got my cell phone back. My parents made their rules very clear: one slipup meant I wouldn't be allowed to ride for the remainder of the season. I was finally off punishment and doing everything I could to make sure I followed every rule they set. I hadn't spoken to Anthony, Abby, and Ms. Julie in three weeks. And Kayla still wasn't talking to me, even when I said hi to her at school. I walked straight to Captain's stall, buried my head in his neck, and breathed in his familiar smell.

"Hi, buddy," I said as he turned to face me and nickered excitedly. Pulling a carrot from my pocket, I admired him as he bit pieces of it from my hand. Captain was the best teacher and teammate, and I had let him down.

"I'm sorry I slacked off and blamed you. I lost my focus for a minute there, but I'll do better, I promise," I whispered to him as he finished his carrot. Then he nuzzled my shoulder as if to say, *"You're forgiven."*

An hour later, I stepped into the arena. Captain

had had a thorough grooming and was as shiny as a penny. I noticed Anthony was finishing up his lesson as I mounted and began my warm-up. He and Ranger looked beautiful as they trotted and cantered around the arena. I had never seen Anthony ride so well before. I suddenly felt very nervous as to how far behind I had fallen. As I walked Captain around the arena, I focused on the skills Grandpa Joe had helped me to perfect.

"Glad to see you back and ready to work, Daija!" said Ms. Julie as Captain and I trotted by. "Anthony, let Ranger walk on a loose rein and cool out."

"You two look really good—even for a warm-up! Sorry for being MIA; my parents took my phone," I said to Anthony as I pulled Captain down to a walk.

"Thanks, Daija, and no biggie!" Anthony said while bringing Ranger from a trot down to a walk.

"But Ranger and I might have to practice a bit more if this is how you'll be riding from now on! Glad you're back, Daija!"

"Hey, do you know if Kayla is here today?"

"Yeah, she has a lesson after you. She's been pretty bummed after you guys had that argument."

"She won't talk to me, and I want to apologize to her."

"She's not mad, just hurt. You two are best friends, and you were pretty rude to her."

Before I could respond, Ms. Julie chimed in, "All right, Daija, let's collect our reins and pick up the trot." I nodded and led Captain around the arena.

As I dismounted after our lesson an hour later, I wrapped my stirrups and led Captain out toward the barn. I wanted to speak with Ms. Julie, but she was already setting up for another lesson, so I planned to talk to her after grooming Captain and doing my barn chores. As I was watering the stalls, I heard Kayla enter with Hershey.

"Hey, Kayla," I said softly, stepping out of a stall.

"Hello, Daija," Kayla said coolly.

"C'mon, Kayla. I'm really sorry for the things I said to you a few weeks ago. You were right about me not being focused, and I was blaming all of my own mistakes on Captain. I know I haven't been the greatest friend to you lately, and I got caught up in trying to fit in. But I took you for granted, and I'm sorry. I also wanted to thank you for being honest with me, even if I didn't want to hear it."

I saw Kayla's eyes soften as I spoke. She sighed before saying, "I accept your apology, Daija. I'm really glad you're back."

"Thanks, Kayla. I really do appreciate you." I wrapped the hose back on its stand before giving her a tight hug. "Now I have to go talk to Ms. Julie."

I felt my nerves rise as I neared Ms. Julie's office door. *Knock, knock!*

"Come on in," I heard her say.

I entered and approached the desk.

"Hi, Ms. Julie," I began shyly.

"Hello, Daija."

"I want to apologize for my behavior. I am really grateful for the chance you've given me. I am sorry that I have not been keeping my word and living up to the expectations that you have of me. I want to be a great rider more than anything, and I know I am capable of doing better—in and out of the saddle."

"Thank you, Daija. I know how hard it is sometimes to do the things we should do instead of the things we want to do. And if you keep riding the way you did today, you and Captain will have no problem earning enough points to qualify for Finals."

Chapter 11
A Second Chance

"Hey, Daija, want to take the boys out on a hack? I haven't taken Khan on the trails in a bit."

I peeked out from around the stack of hay bales to see Abby, bridle in hand.

"Hey, Abby! Sorry I can't today, I need to do some flatwork with Captain. I want to make sure we are solid for Beland."

"Oh, okay," said Abby, looking slightly disappointed. The dust had finally settled with my parents, Ms. Julie, and my friends. I was off punishment and working hard every day to take care of my responsibilities. I didn't want to mess that up now.

I did miss just hanging out at the barn with Abby, Anthony, and Kayla, but with Beland only two weeks away, I wanted to do everything in my power to make sure Captain and I were blue-ribbon ready.

"I did hear some of the other kids tacking up for a trail ride, if you want to go with them."

"Nah, I'd actually rather ride in the arena with you, if you don't mind?"

"Sure! I just have to finish feeding hay," I said, turning back to the stack in front of me.

"I can help you, if you want," offered Abby, before setting her bridle down and helping me fill the wheelbarrows with flakes of hay.

"Thanks, Abby," I said with a smile. Abby and I had begun to develop an actual friendship over the past few weeks, and I no longer dreaded being alone with her; underneath her tough exterior she was a nice girl.

～

From: Daija Williams-Reed
Sent: July 16, 2022, 6:38 p.m.
To: Joe Williams
Subject: Catching you up

Hi, Grandpa!

I hope they are treating you well in the hospital. I'm sorry I can't call you—Mom says you've lost your voice. I miss FaceTiming you, but I don't want you to miss anything, so I thought I'd write to you instead. And hopefully we can talk when you get all better. As you know, Captain and I won first place at Beland, so Anthony, Abby, and I are preparing for Finals. Kayla is sad she won't be competing, but she's been a fantastic practicing buddy! And Captain and I have been doing GREAT and keep improving! I listened to what you said about riding, and I've let everyone know how much I appreciate their support. I wanted to fit in so badly, but I'm learning the only person's approval I need is my own . . . and, of course, Captain's. He doesn't care about what brand of clothes I wear, or how expensive my tack is—as long as I treat him with respect (and feed him lots of treats), he is happy to be my partner.

I got the jacket that Grandma Sheila altered for me! I love it, and I'm going to wear it at Finals next month.

I wish you could come see Captain and me ride. I think you'd be proud of how good we look. I want you to be there when we earn a blue ribbon of our own! I hope you get better soon, Grandpa.

Love, Your Little Cowgirl

Chapter 12
The Final Ride

Our lesson ran late today, so my dad was already in the parking lot waiting for me. As I got into the van, I saw my mom in the front passenger seat.

"Hi, Mom! Guess what!" I gave my parents a play-by-play review of my afternoon as my dad pulled off into traffic. "Captain and I had one of our best lessons to date, and I am beyond excited for Finals tomorrow morning. Ms. Julie kept our lesson light. We focused on fine-tuning my cues, keeping Captain in front of my leg, and keeping him responsive."

"That's good," said Mom, but she seemed distracted.

My dad pulled the car into the driveway, and I raced inside of the house, eager to finish my chores for the night, get my show clothes together, and email Grandpa Joe. As I took off my shoes by the front door, my parents entered behind me.

"Daija, let's have a seat before you settle in," said my dad, leading my mom and me into the living room.

"What's going on?" I asked, looking at my parents. My mom sat silently; she looked like her body was there, but her mind was a million light-years away.

"We have something difficult to tell you, Daija," began my dad. He took my mom's hand in his, before continuing, "There's no easy way to say this . . . Your Grandpa Joe passed away today."

I felt my stomach drop. I couldn't understand what they were telling me.

"I just talked to Grandma Sheila a few days ago. She said he was looking better."

"I know, honey, but I think she didn't want to worry you so close to Finals."

I watched as tears brimmed in my mom's eyes. I didn't know if I should cry or ask questions. How could Grandpa Joe be gone? He was supposed to hear all about Finals. He even said he'd ask Grandma Sheila to FaceTime my parents so they could watch my round. I suddenly felt tired and wanted to take a shower and go to bed.

"I know this is a lot to handle. Your grandpa loved you so much, and he believed in your talent," Mom said.

"If you don't want to ride tomorrow, we

completely understand," added my dad.

I nodded silently as my parents continued to console me. I couldn't manage to do anything else. When they finished, I made my way upstairs to my bedroom. I spotted Grandpa Joe's blue ribbon pinned to my bulletin board. A wave of sadness rushed over me as I touched the ribbon. How could I go to Finals knowing that my grandpa Joe wasn't here anymore?

I reached into my backpack and pulled out my cell phone to text my friends.

> Hey, guys, my grandpa Joe passed away today, so I'm probably going to withdraw from the show. But good luck tomorrow!
>
> 7:41 p.m.

A few seconds later, my phone buzzed with replies, but my heart hurt too much to respond. I turned my phone off and sat in silence for a while. From the moment I began riding with Ms. Julie, I dreamed of joining the North Wind Acres show team, and I dreamed of qualifying for Finals. I climbed into bed, feeling like I had lost not only my grandpa Joe but my dream as well. But Finals seemed insignificant now. I clutched the ribbon tightly in my hands, and the tears began to flow freely.

"I'm going to compete in Finals today," I announced as I finished my breakfast.

"Are you sure? You don't have to. We are proud of you regardless," cautioned my dad.

I nodded my head firmly. I felt sad, but there was a fire in my heart that I couldn't explain. When I finally fell asleep, I dreamed of my grandpa Joe. I saw him in his younger years, jumping effortlessly over the highest jumps. I wanted nothing more than to continue his legacy. Even in my dream, he called me his little cowgirl, and the decision to participate in Finals was the easiest one I had ever made.

"Grandpa Joe taught me to love horses and to trust my horse. I'm sad, but I trust Captain will take care of me over every jump."

"Okay," said my mom firmly, "let's get ready, then."

∽

"Hi, Daija! I'm glad to see you here," said Ms. Julie, appearing behind the North Wind Acres trailer. "I'm sorry about your grandfather. I know it's a tough day, but you are strong, and there's no better therapy than horses."

"Thank you, ma'am," I said softly. I didn't know how else to respond, and all I wanted was to hug Captain and have him take my sadness away.

I walked into the Haverfield barn to find Kayla,

Abby, and Anthony sitting on their tack trunks and sharing a bag of Anthony's mom's granola.

"Daija!" Kayla screamed excitedly, running over to give me a hug. "We weren't sure you were coming."

"Hi, I wasn't sure I was either, but I have to ride for my grandpa."

"I'm so sorry, Daija," said Abby and Anthony, almost in unison.

I gave them a small smile. I was afraid if I kept speaking, the tears I was holding back would fall.

"Here," said Anthony, the bag of open granola outstretched toward me, "have some of my mom's granola. It's good luck."

‿

"All right, everyone! We have twenty minutes until the jumper round. Everyone tack up and give your ponies a final groom before we head over to the warm-up arena!" called Ms. Julie.

Suddenly, everything felt real. In a half hour, I'd be competing in the pony Finals.

"Don't worry, Daija, you'll do great." I turned to see Kayla's warm smile beaming at me. "I'll take care of Captain; you go get dressed."

Having lost her dad, Kayla understood the sadness I felt and made me feel like it would all be okay. As I pulled Kayla into a hug, I felt a familiar nudge on my back. I turned to see Captain staring at me with his deep, soulful eyes. It was as if he sensed the pain and uneasiness inside of me, and he was saying, *"Don't worry, I've got you."* I reached out and stroked his face before turning to head toward the dressing room.

Almost an hour later, I sat atop Captain and waited for our turn to enter the arena. We had jumped clear in the first round, so we'd made it into the jump-off. There were eight riders total in this part of the competition, including Abby. Anthony had been knocked out in the first round.

Captain and I were the last to ride. By the end of our round, I would know if we had won or not. I watched the rider before me get a fifty-three-second time and clear every jump cleanly. Captain and I would have to go fast to beat it.

As Ms. Julie led Captain and me toward the entry gate, she patted my boot and said, "Don't think, Daija, just ride." I nodded my head and shook away any thoughts of fear and doubt. Then I touched my jacket pocket where Grandpa's blue ribbon sat safely, near my heart.

As the bell dinged to signal my start, I asked Captain for a trot, and he surged forward almost instantly—it was almost like he knew how important this ride would be for us. The second bell dinged, and we picked up a canter before turning toward the first jump. As Captain and I raced toward the jump, I pictured the photo of my grandpa Joe jumping and suddenly felt calm. I pushed my hands forward on Captain's neck as we flew over the third jump and whispered, "Okay, boy, let's finish this."

I felt Captain's body tense beneath me and suddenly we were FLYING. We soared over the fourth, fifth, and sixth jumps at a speed I never knew Captain was capable of. I whispered, "Easy," as we continued to move like an express subway train. As we approached the line of final jumps, I heard Grandpa Joe's voice saying, *"Trust your horse."* I exhaled as Captain jumped the line with ease. I heard thunderous applause from the audience and looked up at the clock—51.43 seconds. *WE DID IT!*

As Captain and I cantered around the arena, I smiled the biggest I ever had in my life. I stroked his neck and thanked him over and over for trying so hard for me. I spotted my family in the audience—both my mom and dad were on their feet, clapping excitedly.

As the judges announced my name as the first-place rider, I slowed Captain to a walk to receive our blue ribbon.

Ms. Julie and Kayla were waiting for me at the exit gate, both of their faces beaming brightly. Ms. Julie had tears in her eyes as I dismounted. She hugged me tightly, and I hugged her back.

Kayla jumped on me as soon as Ms. Julie let me go.

"THAT WAS AMAZING, DAIJA! I'VE NEVER SEEN YOU RIDE THAT WAY!"

"Thanks, Kayla. I've never, ever felt that way. Captain was incredible; I owe it to him."

I looked lovingly at Captain, who had dropped his head to graze near our feet, completely unaware of the praise he and I were receiving.

After more rounds of hugs and congratulations, I headed back to the dressing rooms to change.

The North Wind Acres caravan pulled out of the Haverfield grounds lot and headed toward our barn. As I watched trees pass and listened to my family discuss celebration plans, I held my two blue ribbons in my hands and hoped Grandpa Joe was proud of me. I drifted off to sleep as we drove.

⌒

"Daija, we're here," said my mom gently, nudging me in the back seat.

I opened my eyes and headed straight for the trailer to unload Captain.

I removed his dress sheet and thanked him over and over for being the best pony partner I could ever ask for. I stood with him for a minute, brushing his coat and telling him all about Grandpa Joe. Captain stood quietly, ignoring his water and hay, and he let me cuddle and love on him as if he knew I needed the quiet moment. I heard footsteps enter the barn, and suddenly Ms. Julie and my parents appeared at Captain's stall door.

"Daija," began my mom, "we have something for you."

"We are so proud of you," added my dad, "and all the work you have done to prepare for today. You are incredibly strong and dedicated."

"Thank you," I responded to everyone.

My mother pulled an envelope from her pocketbook.

"Here is something to show you how proud we are," she said, handing the small package over to me.

The envelope was heavy in my hand. I opened it and pulled out a folded sheet of paper and a wrapped package. I unfolded the letter and instantly recognized my grandpa Joe's handwriting.

My eyes scanned the words and then suddenly widened in disbelief as I looked up at my parents and asked, "GRANDPA JOE LEASED CAPTAIN?"

My mom nodded, and a tear fell down her cheek and rested on her small smile.

"Your grandma Sheila mailed the letter a few days ago, and we got it this morning."

I unwrapped the package from the envelope and turned the item over in my hands. I looked up excitedly, before returning my eyes to the placard. Engraved on a beautiful gold stall plate were the words CAPTAIN: LOVED BY DAIJA WILLIAMS-REED.

I wasn't sure what to say; all I could do was smile. I felt the familiar nudge at my back, and everyone laughed as Captain nudged me again as if to say, *"No more tears."* I hugged his neck and whispered, *"Finally,* you're all mine."